wood dragon

wood dragon
Copyright © 2019 by Patrick Barney

All rights reserved. No part of this book may be used or reproduced in any form without proper, written permission.

Published by Patrick Barney
Russell, Kansas

ISBN-13: 978-1-7340016-0-0

contents

a tale	5
a daughter	7
worthy suitor	11
unworthy suitor	15
silly little dragon	20
descent to the village	23
selection	31
marriage	39
ascent to the clouds	43
honor & glory	51
invasion	59
a second descent	64
peace	71

a tale

This is an ancient tale – a story from Myaratu – a prestigious land, once found far to the East; its mountain peaks shrouded in the mist of swirling clouds, and territories blanketed by both the conifers of the hill country and the bamboo of its river plains. Located not too far from the borders of Cathay, this land later had interaction with the West, and was visited briefly by Marco Polo and his fellows before its decline.

The origin of the tale is believed to come from Myaratu's early beginnings – that of its first rulers, long before the arrival of the noted explorer from Venice. It was recounted to a travelling merchant who wrote it down and brought it back sometime in the early 1300s to northern Italy. This account was translated into

Flemish and recorded in the *Book of Merchant Adventures* in 1321. It was later included with fables and rhymes in the rare, printed book *Tales from the Orient* from Ghent in 1556.

Although there were at one time various stories that told of the events in this tale, this particular account has survived; and is perhaps the most accurate, it being attributed to Mau Jin – a first line scribe of the royal palace, who purportedly lived at the time of the events.

a daughter

In the second year of the reign of Tonu, Lord of Yause Nograt, was born a daughter to the wife-queen Nulima. The infant was active and healthy and her skin was a clear, ivory sheen that reflected the light in a pearl essence. Her hair was the color of the new moon night, and her infant cries sharp and pointed.

"She shall be a great, ruling monarch and a shield-maiden for sure," her father stated proudly and repeatedly throughout the royal household for many days following her birth.

She was given the label *Storuek* because of her strength, and the name *Karaba*, for she was most beautiful and her radiance flowed upon those who beheld her. Thus in her later life she was known by all as Karaba Storuek – Thundering Rainbow.

- - - -

In the early years of both Karaba's life and that of her family's ruling, it was the usual custom for her family and its entourage to tour the land and pass through villages at the advent of a season of the year. As time passed, this custom waned, until during the adolescent years of the young girl-monarch, when the practice was no more.

It was shortly after this time that Lord Tonu died, and the rule of the realm passed to his closest royal heir, the daughter Karaba. Being only fifteen, the young girl was influenced and assisted by her mother Nulima, the most-favored wife of Tonu.

Intrigue and jealousy pursued the ascent of the young girl to the throne – and it was her mother's obligation to protect and advise her daughter against political traps and even assassination.

It was during the spring, not long after her father's death, that Karaba and her mother met quietly in the gardens behind the palace; with her mother advising her, "You should seek a husband and a strong protector. He should be one who will shield you and see to the needs of the realm – to build it up, and to provide you children to strengthen our bloodline."

For many months, Karaba's mother taught and counselled her daughter as how to reign and rise above the low classes of the people they ruled.

"There shall always be the poor, and they will always pull down light and wisdom, and decline the way of life of those who are honorable and virtuous. Never descend to their lands. Never descend to their habitations. Always look up to the clouds, the skies, and ascend to the stars of the night sky. And if you do so, then you shall lift them (the poor) up."

And in this manner the mother taught her daughter.

- - - -

In her seventeenth year, it was determined that Karaba was prepared and ready to rule on her own.

It was also determined and strongly advised by her mother that her daughter soon select and marry a suitable man – one who would rule at her side. And so, in the summer of that year, a call was made to the landowners, nobility, and royalty not just within the realm, but also of lands both near and far, that Karaba would hold audience at the great hall of the palace and entertain eligible and interested suitors during a two week period immediately following the approaching harvest.

worthy suitor

Upon the first day of presenting potential suitors to the royal house, a large swell of attendants, servants, guards, and impressively arrayed caravans formed a wide and twisted line through the capital city. Hordes of people and animals, both domestic and exotic, thoroughly congested the streets and alleys for days thereafter, but great fortune was granted unto its inhabitants, for the shops and inns were full, and goods and produce were sold in abundance.

The outlying areas were called to help, and villagers and fieldmen from nearby valleys and villages came to assist and to profit from the steadily arriving mass of people.

The early arriving potentials waited patiently until the dawn sun rose fully above the eastern horizon. As it did, the massive palace wall gates opened and the first contender for the royal daughter's hand was allowed to enter. He was a noble warrior lord from a southwestern province of Cathay, and with him came a contingent of twenty-eight elite guards, a battle elephant, and three wagons bearing spoils of his recent conquests. His name was Terfda Khan, and he rode atop his iron clad war beast as he led his complement into the great hall that morning.

"Most impressive!" stated Nulima to her daughter in a satisfying tone.

The great elephant stepped up before the throne and as it did, a company of twelve, silken-clad maidens, wearing the colors of the rainbow, emerged from the first cart and swirled about the pachyderm with torches of fire and shining axes. They danced and swayed across the polished floor and weaved in intricate patterns made mysterious and alive by the waving, fluttering flames. Music of wind and string instruments accompanied and led them during this most amazing mosaic of human movement.

As soon as they finished, a drum sounded loudly, and a tarp was thrown away from the second cart, baring wild and exotic animals, which were then guided by handlers before the throne and the gasping royal women, who were shocked and delighted at the variety and ferocity displayed by such a menagerie.

With the last animal's passing, the third cart was revealed to show treasures obtained from the Khan's latest conquest. The great and most impressive lord descended off his elephant, and from this cart he lifted a large, silver box, which he carried and placed before Karaba of Myaratu.

"This is yours, most beautiful princess."

And as he pointed to the cart – "And the rest, the rest shall be yours – If I am as well!"

He bowed graciously before her and then stood tall and firm. His face was perfect, with a dark brown beard and brown-black hair that ran to his shoulders. His armor covered body accentuated his muscular frame and strong structure. He introduced himself as a warrior and a statesman, and then recited beautiful poetry from the famed Omar Khayyam.

After this, he bowed and took his leave upon his elephant with his entourage following behind.

And this was only the first of many impressive and spectacular presentations that followed – by candidates who sought for the hand of the most beautiful royal daughter Karaba, and thereby gain title to the fertile and prosperous lands of Myaratu – thus adding it to their family honor.

unworthy suitor

For two weeks, the congested and busied atmosphere wore away at the city and its inhabitants, and by the last day, many had feelings of relief and were well looking forward to a rest and the normal flow of life once again.

It was on this last day, in the late afternoon, when it seemed that no candidates for the daughter's hand remained, and with a few moments before the doors were to close at sunset, that a young man walked between the guards and entered the great hall. He was short of stature, simply clothed in earthen toned linen and cotton, and came alone – no attendants or official entourage accompanied him. Stopping a mere few paces from the throne, this young man fell to his knees and prostrated before the daughter and her mother and began to address them.

The mother laughed and interrupted, "You need not bow so before us young one. This is NOT a royal reception before a judging monarch!"

The young man looked up, bewildered and awkward, and slowly rose to his feet.

The daughter, barely holding back her laughter, asked, "So, what is your name and from where do you hail – great noble?"

"I am Aatu Kindo, the son of Huro the noble warrior of the northern border territory Lonsin."

Karaba gave a slight smile. "And?"

"And I am here to ask of you – to find favor with you. To see if you are interested in..." and the young man hesitated and paused. As he did, he quickly looked back and forth at Karaba and her mother.

It had already been a long day, the two royals were worn, and after the many impressive and glorious presentations given before the throne, this last one was akin to a comedy scene; and both women were half-expecting this to be an entertainer hired by one of the previous suitors to impress them one last time. As the young man continued staring, the mother and daughter whispered their suspicions and guesses to each other as to who might have set this up.

Finally, the mother spoke, intending to play along with the joke, "So what have you to offer my daughter? Hmmm? What's in the bag young man?"

Aatu reached into the satchel hanging on his shoulder and pulled out a small, brightly colored object. Karaba stood abruptly and clapped. "Oh, what is it?" she inquired in a mock exhilarated tone.

The young man answer kindly, "A dragon. Made of wood. I made it – for you, Royal Daughter of Tonu. May I?" The girl nodded, and the young man approached the throne and handed it to her.

"It's a very interesting dragon," she stated in an amused tone. She looked at the small beast, which was a brightly colored body of green and orange, painted all over with bluish and green spots, and adorned with reddish toned wings. He had a quirky glance and a slightly mischievous grin. It was a silly gift and compared in no way to the lavish and extravagant presentations and presents the royal daughter had been receiving for days.

The mother was prepared to end the joke, and whispered this to her daughter, but before she said anything out loud, Karaba quietly answered back, "This is no joke. This young man is serious. Look."

And the mother looked at Aatu and noticed his earnest seriousness. She then asked him, "And who again is your father?"

Aatu explained who his father was in detail and how he gained his noble title from her husband. He added that his father had passed the previous year and, upon his death, had given much of the land to his subjects – the people in his charge; and left a small acreage for him, his only son.

The mother spoke loudly to her daughter, "So, this is why you are not soft. This is why you must marry a man who will hold his land and grow and acquire." She then turned to the young man, "And this is all you have to give – because you are poor and destitute."

"No, this is what I give, because I adore your daughter, and I made it with my own hands. It is a gift of me for her."

"That's all very kind and sweet, but what good… is this?" And the mother grabbed the wood dragon and waved it about. "What value is a common piece of timber and shiny pigments? Look, see the array of beautiful craftsmanship from the various regions round about?" And she pointed with the dragon to the mass of gold, silver, and jewelled objects; finely carved, deep wood furnishings; and magnificently worked marble and alabaster.

"This – is a joke!" Then she slapped the wood creature back into her daughter's hand and added, "I think you may go now!"

Seeing his distress and sadness, Karaba quickly spoke up, "He is kind of cute and sassy looking. I like him mother. And Aatu, thank you for the gift. It must have been a great effort for you to make."

The young man silently nodded. He graciously thanked Karaba, bowed to both ladies, and turned and left the great hall with his head down.

silly little dragon

After the closing of the doors, the event ended, and Karaba and her mother headed for the dining hall, to sit, eat, and discuss things. As they walked the passages of the palace, Nulima commented to her daughter, "So why are you bringing that dragon thing? Why didn't you leave it in the hall with all the other gifts?"

The daughter looked down and then realized she was carrying it. "Oh, I don't know – I just wasn't thinking."

"Well, why don't you toss it to one of the servants and have them take it – or dispose of it – or something." And the mother began waving to a maid to come over.

"No, no mother, that's okay. I'll just bring it along. It's sort of cute."

"Dragons aren't supposed to be cute. They're supposed to be powerful – and persistent – and ruthless."

"Yes mother."

The two dined and talked thereafter for a long time at the table about the two weeks of competing suitors and how they would rank each one. After this, they wished each other good night and went to their separate rooms.

Karaba placed the wood dragon on a high shelf, above the boxes of jewelry she kept. She stood back and stared at it. And thought of what her mother had said earlier.

"He *doesn't* look ferocious at all," she said to herself. "Who would make such a dragon?"

Later, as the princess lay down to sleep for the night, the moon shone into the room and poured light onto the wood beast high on the shelf. Karaba couldn't help but notice – and stared at the odd, colorful creature for a while.

"Stop looking at me!" she ordered it. Then she turned herself so as to face the other way. Even so, she imagined that she could feel the dragon looking at her. From time to time she would turn around, and each time, it glared at her with the same, quirky stare. As the night passed, however, she started to fade, her thoughts drifted, and her eyes staying closed longer and longer, and eventually, gradually, she fell asleep.

- - - -

Waking up late the next morning and seeing the sun higher in the sky than usual reminded Karaba of the episode she had had with the dragon. She looked up at the creature with suspicious eyes. It looked back at her the same as it had the night before. It hadn't moved or changed. It simply remained a silly little dragon. The princess made a sneering, growling gesture at it, got out of bed, and called the servants to get her ready for the day.

But that was not the end of it – for during that day, and following two – each time Karaba entered her bedroom, she'd notice the dragon – and it would seem to greet her in its playful silence. By the end of this time, Karaba wanted to know more about this noble – who was this young man that would create such a beast – was he a magician, a sorcerer, an alchemist? What supernatural power did he conjure into such a simple, wood figure? And why? She determined that she must know about this nobleman of the north.

descent to the village

At the advent of night, when the moon was a bright lantern in the low sky, a lone figure stole out a secret passage from the palace and crept silently into the nearby wooded forest. There, a horse awaited, and soon was conveying its rider to the village of Tanagri, located in the northern border province of Lonsin. The way at night was treacherous and steep, but the rider hurried its horse quickly through the forested land, crossing several waters and trekking through stony passages.

Finally, as the moon peeked just over the forest canopy, the sight of the village came into view. Upon arriving at the outskirts of the village buildings, the rider dismounted and tied the horse to a beam under a sheltering roof and proceeded on foot along paths, wandering between buildings, but with a direct course to the walled nobleman's house. At the entrance, the enigmatic figure unveiled her face and bare her head to reveal herself to the guard – who immediately bowed. "Most worthy princess, we are honored. What would you have?"

Karaba answered softly and quickly, "Where is the noble lad Aatu?"

"He is in the far right building, his private workshop."

"I would have that I now enter the grounds, and that you never saw me here."

"So be it princess."

The young royal gave the guard a silver piece, entered the grounds and quickly approached the workshop, located near the wall, and behind a row of mature and densely foliaged pear trees. Light radiated from its open windows, and as she approached, Karaba could hear the noises of scraping and pounding. Coming to one of the windows, she peered inside and saw numerous pieces of finely crafted objects and beautiful carvings of wood around the room. She then noticed the young nobleman working intently on a piece of furniture – a table. She found it curious that a man of noble birth would work in such a manner. It was so base, so common – and quite amusing. Karaba found the entire sight fascinating, for she had never supposed that such a thing could exist. As time went on, and she continued watching in silence as the young lad busily and with fervor continued with the work of a carpenter, she began to feel disappointment and disdain for what he was doing. For what kind of man would he become? And what type of wretched example was he setting for his subjects? Did the guard at the gate know of this activity? And who else might know that this noble leader, this appointed position was being degraded by the peasantish actions of this arrogant youngster?

The young princess soon became enraged and wanted to yell at the insubordinate wretch and his foolish endeavor, but then she thought otherwise. She remembered her status and position to soon become monarch. So she left the open window, and came around to the main door, where she politely knocked and waited.

A voice from inside yelled for her to come in. But she remained where she was – and waited. After a short while, she knocked again, and once again she was bidden to enter. After her third attempt, the door was abruptly opened and left unattended. The princess entered alone and addressed the young nobleman, who immediately turned around, then bowed upon seeing her. As she approached closer, he stuttered and mumbled profuse and numerous apologies. Karaba then laughed loudly and ordered him to rise and face her.

But after Aatu stood, he continued to lower his head, and begged forgiveness for his insolence.

"Don't be silly. You are a nobleman. Do not grovel, do not apologize like a commoner. Now stand up straight young man and face your future queen!" Karaba ordered.

The young man ceased talking and stood up straight before her. As soon as he beheld her face, he was in awe and enchanted by her beauty. His fear and anxiety fled as he was mesmerized by her charming face and delicate features. His expression was obvious, and the princess found his reaction to her, quaint and flattering.

Then she teased him, "Have you never seen me before?" She paused and waited for him to begin to speak – and as he did, she loudly interrupted him, "Ah yes! You were that lowly one at the end of the presentation of the suitors. The one with the colored lizard!"

"Dragon, your highness."

"Ah, yes – the wood dragon. You know, at the time I found him rather impressive. But now that I'm here…" she paused and looked quickly about the workshop, pretending to see his works there for the first time. She continued, "Now that I'm here, I can see that you have accomplished far better, and more worthy projects than my small wood dragon."

Without thinking too carefully, Aatu rashly replied, "But none can compare to the gift I gave you princess!"

"And why is that?"

"I'm sorry – never mind."

"What? What did you say?"

"I'm sorry – never mind. I spoke when I shouldn't have. Please forgive me."

"Forgive you? For what? What is so special about my silly wood dragon?"

Aatu stood silent and looked down.

Karaba insisted, "Now, what is so special about it? Speak up."

Aatu looked up at Karaba and softly replied, "I am fearful to speak, for I do not seek to offend you."

The princess smiled, then shook her head. "You are a simple noble – you shall not offend me – now speak."

Aatu began, "When I was young and in my twelfth year, I saw you and your family pass through my village. Your procession stopped and your father spoke with mine for a short while, and as he did, I beheld your face and you were beautiful and glorious. I remembered and thought of you the entire day thereafter, and that night I had a dream. In it, I saw an evergreen, tall and stately. And as I approached, it leaned and fell toward me, and as its trunk touched the ground, the whole of it transformed into a colorful dragon of green and orange, with reddish wings, a searching glance, and a slight smile. He spoke to me, 'Lad, I shall warm and open her heart to you!' And then my dream ended. I knew the dragon spoke of you, and I was hopeful and excited and felt a longing and passion for your affection.

"I arose that morning and spoke with my father of my dream, and he took me to the workshop and had the carpenter there show and teach me how to work the wood. At the end of the month, I had formed and created a small, wood dragon; and with the assistance of the potter, I learned how to decorate and paint my work. When I had finished it, I took it to the woods near my house and held the dragon close to me and prayed that it might contain my heart and my love for you.

"I intended to give you my dragon the next spring visit, but your family never came again, and so I kept it, wishing and hoping for a time to give it to you."

The princess was faintly moved and thought it a somewhat nice tale. She replied in an official tone, "Well, thank you for the gift. I shall always treasure it."

Karaba looked at Aatu with condescending and doubtful eyes, turned her gaze about the room again at the various objects and pieces Aatu had created, and then looked back at him and said insistently, "Tell me about all these things you've made. I'd like to hear."

And Aatu eagerly began to share with her and explain pieces he had made and what he was planning to do.

And she listened carefully, for she was

amused and fascinated by him – and why someone of noble birth would stoop so low as to make such things.

After Aatu had talked about and shared a small portion of his works, Karaba yawned loudly.

"Oh, the night is growing late – and I must go now. Perhaps we shall meet again young nobleman." And with that, the princess stepped forward, patted the young man's shoulder, and abruptly left without another word.

selection

During the next few weeks, there was a hurried and frenzied mood about the royal palace, for twelve suitors had been chosen to meet and spend time with the princess. Each chosen man would have three days to reside at the palace and be with the wife-queen and her daughter. Servants and guards were prepared and readied, the grounds were acutely and finely manicured, and structures and buildings freshly painted. The palace was immaculate and the princess was outfitted with a fresh, new wardrobe of thirty-six changes of attire.

The twelve potentials were all valiant and warrior nobles who had proven themselves in battle and had increased their families' landholdings.

The two months previous to Karaba's

coronation were set up for this selection process. If a suitable man were chosen, then he would be announced and presented to the people on that day, with the royal marriage to take place the following month.

During this selection, after each visit there was a two-day break, and at that point, Karaba would retire each night to her room and upon seeing the wood dragon, would think again about Aatu. And each time, very early the next morning, she would escape from the palace and journey to the residence of the young nobleman.

Each time she arrived, he would be in his workshop, busily engaged on a project of some sort. She enjoyed being there, for she found it comfortable and an open atmosphere. She thought Aatu was amusing and found his ways common, but she also liked his manner; and although she had mixed feelings about him, she was mysteriously drawn to him. She couldn't seem to keep herself away.

As the time progressed, Aatu realized that his initial hope for her love was probably not likely. She, in her manner to him, seemed more like a near relative. They would often spend time with her quietly watching while he worked, or lightly talking during his breaks, but she would never touch his work or tools, as though she had to keep her distance from what he did in his workshop.

At the end of each time they were together, Karaba would very politely thank her host for his company, and the tea and refreshment he provided.

Karaba never told her mother of these times she spent with Aatu.

On the final day of the princess' visits to Aatu, and shortly before her coronation, Karaba thanked the young noble as usual, but this time handed him a small silver token, and said, "Now Aatu, I will not be coming back to visit you here anymore. I will be officially queen in two days, and at that time I shall name who will be the ruling noble and my future consort. I want you to be there, for I will have something special to give to you. Give this coin to a royal attendant, and you shall be given a special place to sit."

Upon saying this, the princess smiled and quickly turned and left, before Aatu could properly reply.

- - - -

The day of Karaba's coronation was a beautiful and grand affair. The palace and its grounds were aflame with yellow and green banners. The royal temple was freshly adorned with new flowering plants and artistically trimmed trees and bushes.

Many of the nobility from the provinces arrived one or two days in advance with grand processions, accompanied by attendants, priests, and soldiers. The more esteemed and higher ranked officials were granted housing and accommodation in the royal palace.

The capital city was alive with activity and there were rumors and stories all about as to whom would be chosen as the consort to the queen that day.

At noon, one hundred trumpeters sounded for all to gather upon the square before the palace wall and the temple grounds, where the official ceremony would take place. Along the two front rows were places for the members of the royal family and their closest companions. The next two rows were reserved for the highest and most esteemed nobility of the realm. This is where Aatu was seated—directly behind Princess Karaba's closest cousins. As he sat, he noticed the cousins glancing back at him, talking among themselves and giggling. He couldn't quite hear all of what they were saying, but he was sure he heard the word "dragon" used many times.

As more and more people filed in and were seated, Karaba, covered in a simple robe, privily approached Aatu and placed something into his hand. She whispered, "Here, this is something special for you." And then she hurried away.

Aatu looked down and saw it was an object wrapped in a silk cloth. It was heavy and felt jagged and pointed. As he opened the cloth, he saw a handwritten note, which said:

*To Nobleman Aatu of
Lonsin Province -
Here is a royal dragon,
a proper dragon.*

After further unwrapping the beautiful cloth, he beheld a most magnificent piece of work. It was a dragon with an open mouth and sharp claws. It was most ornate and opulent – finely crafted of gold and jade with embedded emeralds as eyes, and ruby highlighted wings. Its body was curled and twisted and its wings folded, but ready to open. It was indeed a royal and a very proper beast.

Aatu was impressed with the gift, but wasn't sure what it meant, and why Karaba had given him this. He was hopeful of something wonderful that day, but was in no way sure.

- - - -

At the time for the ceremony to begin, the trumpeters sounded again, this time for a prolonged period; followed by a series of drum beatings, and then a jubilant choir of priests and holy attendants.

Immediately following the singing, a deep and solemn chanting ensued, and it was during this that Karaba and her mother walked among the nobility gathered in the square. They did not take a direct route to the throne, but instead wandered among the people, who held out their hands so that the future queen might touch them as she passed.

As Karaba neared the throne, a great priest also approached, holding a golden rod and a steel sword before him. The two met before the throne, and as Karaba grasped both items in her hands, the priest began a holy incantation, and the choir lowered their voices and turned their cloaks to reveal colors of the sunbird. The words recited by the priest were of an ancient tongue that most there could not understand, but the rhythm and the cadence were solemn and glorious, and seemed to carry a special weight and holiness – a power from the heavens.

Aatu was moved and cried as he watched Karaba, the most beautiful one to him, become queen, for he sensed her specialness. And from that moment forth, he felt a strong and eternal allegiance and loyalty to her.

After the great priest ceased, he bowed and released his hands, giving the rod and sword wholly to the girl who was now queen.

The audience cheered, and Karaba turned to the crowd and raised her arms and smiled. As the sounds and congratulations from the cheering people waned, Karaba's mother stood by her side, then raised her voice, "And now comes the marriage announcement that many of you have waited for and looked forward to. My daughter will now present the worthy lord who shall be by her side – who shall be the strengthening arm of this country!"

Nulima then stepped to the side and Karaba spoke loudly, pointing her sword to her left,

"The future lord and protector of Myaratu and the husband who shall be by my side is this great and warrior noble!"

A curtain was drawn, revealing Terfda Khan, who stepped forward and then across an elevated stone walk to Karaba, where she reached out and both of them wielded the steel sword of her coronation. The audience cheered and drums and trumpets sounded. Nobles and royalty talked and conversed enthusiastically among themselves, and there was great jubilation and joyousness in the square. And it could almost be said that all that were there were happy.

But there was one who was not.

marriage

A month passed, and on the day of her marriage, Karaba rose up early in the morning and called her maidservant to the room. She had assembled her jewelry boxes and other valuable objects upon a short table near her bed.

When the servant girl arrived, the queen directed her, "Take these things and place them in the rosewood chest, the one over by the window."

Then she pointed to the things left on the shelves near her bed. "And those things, well, just throw them out – get rid of them." With that, the queen left the room to go bathe.

After the maidservant had put the valuable items carefully away in the chest, she began quickly clearing the other objects off the shelves, tossing them into a pile; and while she did, she paused and held onto one particular item and looked at it carefully – the brightly colored wood dragon.

- - - -

The wedding was a magnificent affair; and statesmen and dignitaries from all over the realm attended. The palace, temple, and administrative buildings were adorned with flowers and beautiful banners, and the people were festive in appearance and temperament. No detail was left unnoticed, and the opulence and merriment of the occasion lifted the spirits of all who attended.

The ceremony was performed in the late morning, leaving the afternoon and evening to be filled with festivals and events that carried on throughout the capital well past midnight; although the married pair escaped the crowds much earlier, retreating without announcement through the winding passages of the palace.

"We shall ascend to the clouds," proclaimed the new ruler Terfda Khan to his blushing bride while he carried her to her room from the outer passage. As he stepped near the bed, Karaba instinctively looked at the top shelf, expecting to see her silly little dragon friend – but he wasn't there. She paused in thought, wondering where it had gone, and then remembered earlier that morning. The Khan noticed the lost look in his new wife's eyes and asked what it was.

She turned to him. "Oh, nothing, just something I remembered about this morning; but nothing important."

"Good, I wouldn't want my dearest one to be troubled; for now the promise of the world is ours to take, and we and our offspring shall inherit all that we desire." And he looked deeply, passionately into Karaba's eyes. She melted from the power of his embrace and trembled at his strength and beautiful countenance. She felt weak and hesitated, and thought of asking him to have leave for a brief moment; but he continued holding her securely in his arms as he placed her onto the bed. He rashly tore away her outer robe and held her in an embrace that stole away her breath.

She was his, and he was to take her. He touched and moved upon her body as a hungry wolf; his presence was as iron, and his dominant bearing secure and sure. She looked upon him and smiled, realizing she was now the wife of a warrior, a conqueror's queen, and felt that all that would happen – now and in their future – would bring her happiness, honor, and glory. And although frightened and nervous that night, Karaba willingly submitted herself in all to her husband, for he was the great Terfda Khan.

ascent to the clouds

Myaratu rose to a great power under the Khan's leadership, for he acquired mineral-rich lands in the east, secured and stabilized the borderlands, and established advantageous trade and political alliances.

Years passed and in the spring of the sixth year of marriage, Karaba had still not conceived. It was at this time that Terfda Khan began to stay away from his wife at night, and also began the renovation of one of the palace buildings. When Karaba asked her husband where he went at night, or where he slept, he would simply smile and kiss her forehead.

Then one day, he arrived at the palace early in the morning with two accompanying carts full of young women. They were taken to the courtyard near the newly renovated building –

the garden house. Once there, their clothing was removed and Terfda and his first attendant carefully looked them over. From this, ten were chosen and given new clothes, with the remainder sent away.

Karaba heard of these women from her maidservant later in the afternoon, and rushed to the garden house, only to see her husband talking and laughing with a couple of them, reclining on cushions. She stood at the doorway and called his name. He slowly and politely excused himself from their presence while his wife waited, and once outside, she demanded to know what was happening.

"Well, these are my women," Terfda Khan casually replied.

"What do you mean?"

He looked at her and smiled. He wasn't going to answer her further, nor did he need to. He was the Khan of Myaratu – and it was then that she realized his status and position, and what she was to him. She apologized for her rude manner, and turned and quickly left, running away.

Karaba was desperate and scared and had not realized until that moment her true situation in life. She cried in anguish, and sought solace from her mother, whom she found in an annex room, preparing herbs for medicine.

"Dear mother, what can I do? There are new women in the palace. They are young and beautiful. And they are my husband's. And I heard that more will probably be coming soon."

Her mother looked at her with surprise, then continued with handling the herbs.

"Mother!" Karaba insisted.

"What am I to say? You married a great warrior, as did I. And great warriors desire great things. Has he not provided you with what you desire?"

Karaba said nothing, but looked questioningly at her mother.

"Daughter Karaba, you married a warrior – a great noble – and great men always require many things. Did you think that you would be enough? Karaba, no single woman is ever enough for a great man. It has always been this way – and always will be."

"So is there nothing I can do?"

"Of course there is – always be the favored one. I told you this before – and many times – did you not listen? You know of your father and the many women he had. Did you think your marriage would be any different?"

Karaba looked down and lowered her shoulders. Her mother placed what she had on the table and held her daughter close.

"Be strong, and bear him strong children, and you shall always be the favored one in the household." And Nulima taught and instructed her daughter further as to what she should do, and how she could satisfy her husband more in bed, so that she would stay in his favor.

However, as the months passed and the queen still had not conceived, her husband stayed longer and longer away from her, spending most of his nights in the garden house; and other times away with friends on treks of hunting and adventure.

- - - -

The new year came, and with it also the loneliness and the heartache that Karaba felt in losing her husband to his concubines. On the second day, she opened her rosewood chest and while sitting, looked through the many items she had treasured as a child. As she lifted a beautiful silk scarf, it unrolled and from it tumbled a wood creature softly onto some cloths.

"The dragon!" Karaba said out loud. "How did it get here?" She yelled out the name of her maidservant, and when she arrived, the queen inquired of it.

The servant answered, "I know you told me to throw it away long ago, but when I looked carefully at it, there was an inscription on the bottom, and I figured you'd probably want to keep it. Maybe you had forgotten it on the shelf – and since you were in the bath, I didn't want to bother you, and it was so small anyway, it didn't take up any space. I'm sorry, did I do wrong?"

Karaba looked kindly at her maidservant and smiled warmly. "No, no you didn't. You did right. Thank you. You may go."

After the servant left, Karaba quickly got up and put the colorful wood dragon back in its usual spot on the shelf.

- - - -

In mid-spring, word came by courier to the palace that the eastern frontier was threatened by a bandit army, supported by the neighboring country. Terfda Khan was absent that day, apparently reviewing the border guard and troops in the southwest, so the action to be taken fell to Karaba's orders. She had never commanded military action on her own, so she sought the counsel of her mother.

"Send messengers to all ten provinces, requiring the nobles to send one thousand soldiers each, and that each command be led by a high noble, and be here within a week. Accept nothing less. This will secure you as a solid and formidable leader. With this, your honor shall ascend to the clouds."

Karaba did as her mother advised and sent the order. But two days later, the messenger sent to the northern province of Lonsin returned with the following reply:

We are fully aware of the bandit incursion in the east—but the numbers and leadership you request of the provinces far exceeds the remedy required.

Know that now in the north is our planting time and many men are required to prepare the land and complete tasks.

Respectfully, we shall provide one hundred well-trained archers and their captain to arrive at your capital in five days' time.

All the nobles of our province are required to remain, as they are needed to direct the planting and sowing activities.

> *With honor & respect*
> *Noble servant Aatu Kindo*
> *Lonsin Province*

After receiving and reading the letter, Karaba brought it to her mother, who then advised her daughter to arrest the traitorous nobleman, destroy and level his residence to the ground, and appoint a new noble, preferably someone young and from the capital city. Karaba fully agreed and said she'd take care of it in the morning.

- - - -

In the evening, as Karaba prepared herself for bed, she noticed the small wood dragon on the shelf. She walked up to it and stated, "Your master will be imprisoned and probably killed.

What about that? You think that's something to smile about? Well?"

And the dragon continued smiling.

Karaba turned and then went to bed. As she lay there, she looked up at the dragon again – and as she did, she began to think. And she remembered something her servant girl had said about an inscription on it. Karaba then got up and brightened a lantern. She went over to the dragon, took it off the shelf, and turned it over to read what it said:

> *Karaba, you are the only girl for me – there shall be no other. Aatu*

honor & glory

The army assembled from the ten provinces was formidable, and it marched to a complete victory, not only destroying the bandits, but also conquering the half of the lands of the country that supported them. Many soldiers died and there was an enormous cost involved, but the acquired territory was a glorious prize and an honor for Karaba. After Terfda Khan returned, he praised his wife most vehemently, but still spent most of his nights in the garden house, away from her.

Her mother, Nulima, was also proud of her daughter's victory. When she inquired of Karaba pertaining to that rebellious noble Aatu in the north, she replied, "Aatu who?" to which her mother laughed loudly.

That next winter was harsh, and the cold

was bitter in the capital city. Many people became ill and died. And during the last month, Nulima suffered from a severe lung ailment and soon passed away. The household mourned, but only for a short while, because the time was fast approaching for a new era in the realm. An era that was to be ushered in by the great warrior lord Terfda Khan.

- - - -

"We shall rule all the lands that border upon us!" was the proclamation spoken by the great Khan of Myaratu on the day of the new year. It was soon thereafter written and then posted throughout the villages and territories of the realm.

The armies of the lord would become powerful, and the prizes and rewards promised to those who served honorably and valiantly were great. Many landworkers and servants were encouraged to leave their posts of lowly status to join up with the army – to ascend to the clouds.

The season for war was soon to come, and myriads of preparation were taking place throughout the realm. Smiths and armorers were busy working metal and preparing for soldiers' gear. Horses and other beasts were being trained and equipped for battle, and a new line of officers and noble warriors were in the processes of training and initiation.

When the rivers that flowed from the northern mountains ran swift from the snow melt, Terfda Khan made the call to war, ordering the provincial troops to assemble and and ready themselves for action.

Most of the soldiers were called to the capital, but for two provinces, the orders were for their soldiers to stay and prepare. One of these was Lonsin, the northern province. The snow was still deep in the mountain passes there, so their mission would have to wait.

On the day of the spring equinox, Terfda Khan led his army south on its first expedition – and one which engulfed his country and people in a series of conflicts that would rage on for years.

Two months after the Khan's forces left for the south, the northern province of Lonsin was ordered to advance, conquer, and then occupy the Labbak tribal lands to the north.

At first the victories in the south were swift and decisive. The southern lands were ill-prepared and unaware of the force and tactics they were to face. But with time, other countries allied together and obtained information to better protect themselves. Intricate fortifications and defenses were devised, and so battles became longer and protracted, and diseases afflicted more and more in the field.

Terfda Khan's two-year plan for his army to succeed soon became three, and then four years. After the fifth year, the lord of Myaratu established fortifications then returned to his palace for a rest. As he arrived, a smiling Karaba was there to greet him, but he did not notice or acknowledge her, for he returned in the company of three of his women, whom he had sent for while in the field; and was drunk and busily engaged with them upon his arrival.

Karaba, upon seeing this, turned and fled to her room, where she took the wood dragon and held it close to her heart as she fell to her bed, and then wept bitterly.

- - - -

After a year-long respite at the palace, Terfda Khan again addressed his country and made a call to arms. Repeating what he said before and offering the same to those who would join the fight, the people admired and respected their leader, who had already expanded their realm to almost double its initial size.

The night before Terfda Khan was to leave, Karaba approached him and begged him to stay with her that night. He kissed her forehead tenderly and said resolutely, "Dear Karaba, you can bear me no children."

"My lord, I am your wife, and the queen of Myaratu. Besides, these women can give you no royal heirs."

"But I am a warrior, and they *can* give me warrior sons!"

And so, on the final night before his departure, Terfda Khan stayed in the garden house with his many women.

- - - -

The assembled army was now double that of before, and the lord of Myaratu was confident in this campaign. He led his force this time to the east, crossing the swollen rivers, thus surprising his enemies and easily subjugating their forces; and then turning them to fight for him. He led his soldiers to the south and headed westward, easily sweeping across the expanse of open fields and desert areas within a year.

Upon reaching the western countries, Terfda Khan offered surrender to the three tribes that occupied the area. They refused and fought valiantly and ferociously before they fled and vanished into dense forests. It was shortly after this that Terfda Khan fell grievously ill and died. The leadership of the army fell to the first advisor, who hesitated and wavered as to what to do next. So half the army disbanded and most of these soldiers returned home. The remaining army was then stationed in the south – to organize and secure newly acquired territories.

Word reached home of the Khan's death and the country mourned for a month. Karaba was now the only royal leader of the Myaratu – responsible for all of the administrative, civil, legal, and military affairs of the country. During the reign of the Khan, she had excused herself from most of such official activities, allowing her husband to direct and control things. Almost all of the advisors and bureaucratic staff were affiliated with her husband's tribe and kin, and showed little loyalty to her. The recent, large expansion of the realm required a massive undertaking to control, and Karaba had no experience or connections, no one close to help her. Except one, there was one who would surely help her – Aatu.

She sent messengers and a royal escort to the village of Tanagri to bring Aatu back. But two days later, the messengers returned with no one. Karaba asked where he was, to which she was told he had died – burned in a fire the year before. Karaba cried and mourned for days, and did not eat. It was reported that she was seen in her apartment – walking back and forth, talking to herself and holding a small wood creature in her hands. Some thought she was going mad. Others said it was the loss of her husband – and she just needed more time.

But time was not on Karaba's side, for word of the Khan's death spread quickly not just within the realm, but also throughout the surrounding, enemy lands; and some saw this as an opportunity to strike back.

Rumors of an uprising in the west reached the palace and Karaba decided to send a strong expeditionary force of elite soldiers from the capital to scout and settle in the area. This band would be supplemented by the army that was stationed in the south. Her numerous advisors tried to dissuade her, citing the costs and the danger of moving so many soldiers from protecting the palace and southern lands. But she was unmoved, for she had consulted with a soothsayer, who claimed the advice had come from her deceased mother.

So the forces were sent in the late fall, leaving the capital city with few to defend it.

invasion

Ten days before the winter solstice, invading enemy forces from the south crossed the wide and swift running Hinju River and made their march swiftly toward the capital city. There was no one in the south to oppose them, for the army had been unwisely sent to the western frontier.

Seeing the desperate and futile situation created by her own pride and stubbornness, Karaba summoned her elite royal cohort to stand guard at the walls of the palace, and there they waited for their enemies' arrival.

Meanwhile, Karaba sent swift messengers to her forces in the western lands to call them back; and also prepared for her own escape, knowing all too well that reinforcements would likely be too late.

When the enemy army under Idran Khan descended upon the capital city, they burned much of the wooden buildings to the ground and killed many of the animals and livestock. They corralled women and children and systematically carted them away as slaves.

Their approach to the fortification of the royal palace was slow and deliberate, taking many days. Trumpeters were presented at the front of the infantry, blaring their instruments throughout the day. And at night, brightly burning torches – their rising smoke and drifting ash choking the deep black sky – illuminated the city's bleak state. This was done to intimidate and demoralize the defending force of the palace, but had the opposite effect – for Karaba Storuek rallied her troops and lifted up their spirits. "Do not despair, but be glad of the enemies' slow approach, for it gives time to our army in the west to come for us."

On the afternoon of the day before the new moon, the leader of the enemy rode to the wall to call out terms of surrender. He was accompanied by four riders, two on either side, wielding pikes with the severed heads of all the messengers Karaba had sent west.

"Here is your message of salvation, Queen!" called out the sure and smiling Khan. "Here are your words, still bound within their minds and mouths. Should I release them back to you? Perhaps you may give them a different message this time." He paused and looked carefully at the guards atop the wall – so he could witness and savor their fallen and distraught countenances. He continued, "Give up your Queen, and we shall spare half your lives. You have until sunrise to decide."

Then the Khan yelled to those riders who were with him. They planted their pikes into the ground, then swiftly rode away with their master to retire to their camp – to celebrate loudly, while the palace guard and Karaba suffered in anguish at the sight of an inevitable defeat.

- - - -

At sunrise, as the soldiers of Idran Khan arose, they found many of their army dead – their throats slashed. Many called out and cried, and others were angry and wanted rashly to fight right away – to quickly avenge the deaths of their brothers.

Idran Khan was shocked, but impressed;

and amid the confusion of his troops, he was able to organize and issue commands to his captains, who were then able to calm and rally the soldiers together.

Within a short time, they were instructed, prepared, and then hurried off to complete their tasks. But no soldiers approached the palace – no attack was made. Those at the palace wall were mystified – and nervous; for the enemy forces scattered throughout the city and into the bordering forest, keeping far away from the palace walls. This continued the entire day.

By evening, the soldiers had all returned to their camp and were busily engaged in doing something. As the night grew late, great fires were lit and flames were seen dancing about the camp. Noises and cheering could be heard for a short while, and then it became very still and quiet, and activity in the enemy camp seemed to cease. There was no moon to be seen in the sky, and few stars were visible through the blanketing clouds.

Suddenly fires ignited all around the palace wall, followed by sounds of movement, and soon a thousand fires could be seen dancing about. Then calls were made and the flames hurled through the sky and into the palace compound. The flying arrows struck roofs and trees, and fires erupted. Again and again, one after another, sets of arrows, each having at least a thousand flaming tips, landed upon the palace buildings and its grounds.

Many within the walls hurried about to put out fires. Most were successful, but some fires caught quickly and burned intensely. Karaba saw smoke coming out of her apartment window, and rushed to get inside. An attendant noticed what she was doing and grabbed her arm right before she entered. She called out to let go, and tore her arm away, then pushed the man back as he tried to stop her again.

"I have to get my dragon!" she screamed as she ran into the smoke-filled doorway. Soon after, there was a terrible crash as the roof fell on top of Karaba, and several people ran in to rescue her.

a second descent

When Karaba opened her eyes, she was lying on her back, with a white linen sheet covering her. By her side sat her royal physician.

"Where am I?" she asked.

"You are in the garden house. And you are safe."

"What happened?"

"The army came and rescued us. You're safe now."

"But why am I here?"

"The palace roof fell on you, and you were injured."

Then Karaba remembered what had happened. She looked around desperately.

"Where is it?"

"Where is what?"

"My dragon."

"Oh, that – well, it's right here." And the physician picked up the wood creature from off the floor and handed it to her.

"Thank you. Thank you," she said relieved.

"It must be something special – you risked your life for it. We found you with it under the debris. You were holding it tight with both hands."

"It is something special." And Karaba lay back down and closed her eyes, gently holding the dragon.

- - - -

Later, Karaba learned that one of the messengers who had been caught, had convinced a close friend along the way to travel with him. When the messenger was captured, the friend fled away and informed the armies to return to the capital. The soldiers arrived just before dawn, annihilating the invading army, and killing their leader. It was counted as a victory for Karaba, and when she was told that a great celebration would be held in her honor, she adamantly refused.

During her recovery, Karaba had teams of advisors inform and counsel her of the many affairs of the realm that had to be managed and addressed. The capital city had to be rebuilt. The territories secured. Taxes needed to be collected; and other funds secured to pay the military and rebuild the palace. Almost all the territories were short in their agricultural production, because of the loss of men in war and the resulting lack of able workers.

Soon, Karaba was back on her feet, but she felt lame. She was inadequate for what was ahead of her, and she knew that she did not deserve to lead. And also, she feared for her life. She privately spoke with an advisor who was her father's nephew, and obtained vital information from him. She found out that Lonsin was the only province prospering at the moment. It was also the safest militarily and the most loyal to her. And it turned out that Lonsin never did invade the northern tribes as directed by her late husband. Instead, they established trade and cultivated political ties, which prospered both areas and established a lasting peace. This came about because of

Aatu's wise leadership, which was carried on by his cousin – who now ruled.

- - - -

Over several days, Karaba planned with this advisor for her to secretly travel to the north, coordinate with the noble there for military leadership, and then travel to the northern tribes to ask for relief and assistance in securing and rebuilding Myaratu. She would then seek sanctuary and live in exile somewhere in the north, and the realm would be turned over to her father's brother's son Baktul, who would have the support of a military led by loyal, northern officers. After the plan was set, Karaba rode off on her own to the north, dressed as a peasant.

Although it had been years since she'd travelled to Tanagri, she remembered the way well. When she arrived, it had changed. There were now beautiful stone buildings and neatly ordered streets. A large canal of fresh water ran along the roadway that led to the town center. Beautiful carved bridges adorned the waterways, of which there were not a few. And the population seemed to have swelled to many times what it had been when she was there before.

Karaba thought of Aatu and what greatness he had accomplished. She rode through the busy and active streets up to the noble residence, which looked exactly the same. She announced who she was and was given immediate entry. Once inside the wall, she noticed a new building, where Aatu's workshop once stood. She dismounted her horse and walked over to it, where she heard some noises inside. She peered through an open window and saw a man, busily working on a piece of rough cut timber.

"Aatu!" she called out, but when the man turned, she realized it was someone else.

He replied, "I'm sorry, my name is Dakken, I'm Aatu's cousin, and the ruling noble. And you are?"

"I am Karaba Storuek–your queen."

Immediately the nobleman bowed and greeted her in a most official way.

Karaba then told the purpose of her visit, and that in the morning she would journey to the north countries. He invited her to dine with him and his wife in the main residence, and there they discussed the details of her plan.

- - - -

In the morning, against the advice of her noble host, Karaba set off alone on foot for the north pass. The trail was too treacherous for horses; and the winter snows could come and accumulate in the high country, so she had to hurry. But the queen was determined, for time was short, and relief and help for her people was needed sooner than later.

As she travelled along steep and winding paths, the fresh, cool air and breeze was refreshing. The journey would take at least three days to the border hut and the mountain pass, so Karaba would have to sleep outside a couple nights. She had never done such a thing before. The first night went well, but during the second, she was accosted by bugs, beetles, and mosquitoes. Sounds and noises reverberated throughout the night, awaking and frightening her. She awoke tired and disoriented; and at first, she started down the trail in the wrong direction.

In the morning of this, her third day, snow began falling, and as she climbed higher, not only did the snow become heavier, but she was walking on thick layers of snow and ice. As the afternoon progressed, the temperature seemed to drop and she found herself in snow that reached to her knees. When the late afternoon sun was slightly above the mountain ridge to the west, Karaba became worried. She figured she should have reached the border hut by now, and there was nothing in sight. Before her were jagged stone faced cliffs and vast sheets of snow and ice. She became tired and wanted to rest a short moment, but there was no proper shelter. She finally decided to rest near a short evergreen tree, and close her eyes for just a moment.

peace

"Karaba, Karaba!" The queen heard her name being called, so she opened her eyes and looked across a dark, snowy expanse, dimly lit by a shrouded moon. The snow had ceased falling, and the chill of the air was lessened because of the now stilled wind.

"Am I dreaming?" she thought. She wasn't sure, for she didn't feel the cold, nor did she feel the desperation as she had before she slept. She looked across the pure, smooth, and blanketed white field ahead and thought perhaps this was death, because she was now at peace – for she felt a particular calm as she gazed upon the stillness around her.

Then she saw a brief reflection of light on a snow covered slope in the distance. She looked up to see the pale moonlight behind the blanketing clouds – it was too weak to form such an occurrence.

Once again, she saw a flicker of light coming off the snowy slope. She got up and stepped through the deep white frozen mass, determined to see what it was that might cause this light. As she approached the slope, she saw smoke rising above the thinning forest of trees.

"A house!" she spoke aloud to herself. "The border hut – it must be that." And she quickened her pace through the knee deep snow. As she headed toward the smoke, she saw tiny sparkles of light and soon thereafter the faint outline of a building. The forest growth waned until she was standing upon a small snow covered meadow, with the border hut just a short distance away. Through a window, she could see movement inside. Tired, numb, but full of excitement, Karaba called out. Soon a door opened, and the queen eagerly hurried her steps to meet the person who was there.

She stumbled several times right in front of the hut, unable to properly find the snow-covered stairs that led up to the door. After her fifth fall, she stayed down and called out in frustration. She tried to get up again, but then slipped back down into a sitting position. She wanted to yell out, but found herself weak and her voice failing. She remained where she was, just a few paces from the hut, and cried bitterly.

Soon she felt something gentle and powerful grasp firmly under her arms and lift her up. Then she was completely carried off the snow and conveyed by a strong, bearded man into the warm and well-lit habitation.

Once inside, she looked around and saw an array of finely crafted furniture, carved wood objects, and curious statues and figurines. And then she saw a silly looking creature.

"That's my dragon!" she exclaimed.

The border guard put Karaba carefully down into a chair next to a table. As he turned and headed to the oven, she quickly reached into her satchel and pulled out her own wood dragon. Surprised and confused, she turned to see the guard, who was pouring heated water.

"Where did you get that dragon?" she asked.

"Which one?" he softly replied.

She turned to look at the wood figurine again, but this time noticed another creature right next to it. This was also a dragon, but it was ornate and opulent – finely crafted of gold and jade with embedded emeralds as eyes, and ruby highlighted wings.

"Uh, both of them," she answered, while staring at them.

Silently, the border guard placed a tankard of warm tea on the table next to the queen. He then walked around and pulled a chair closer to her, sat down, and simply said her name, "Karaba."

And suddenly she knew. She turned and looked carefully at the man. She saw through his roughened, bearded face and looked into his eyes. His pure, loving, and endearing eyes.

"Aatu," she gasped. "How, how – are you alive? How are you here?"

Aatu smiled. "I guess I hadn't died yet."

Karaba leaned to him and placed her hands upon his shoulders and shook him gently. "Is it you? Are you real?"

"Yes. Yes I am. But first, you should drink this and warm yourself up. You need your strength."

"Yes, yes, you're right." And Karaba released Aatu and began sipping her tea.

Aatu then spoke, "You know, I'm equally surprised to see you now. How did you come here – and why?"

Between sips, Karaba explained what had happened to her and the realm, and the journey she had taken to secure help from his cousin; and then her intention to go to the north, plead for help, and then to live in exile – to start anew as a stranger in a place where she would not be known.

After she completed her account, Aatu got up and filled her cup again with tea. He then walked over to the shelf, picked up the wood dragon Karaba had asked about, and came back with it. He placed it on the table next to hers.

He began, "First, I want you to know that in my heart and mind, I was never disrespectful of you, my queen. I was always honorable in my service and defense of our people."

Karaba looked at Aatu tenderly, and placed her hand on his, and spoke, "I know Aatu. I know you are honorable; but I didn't always know – for at one time I was prepared to have you seized, and strip away your title and land. But something stopped me – something that was at first slight and small, and slowly grew over time. Something that is in the meaning of this." And Karaba placed her other hand on her dragon, then looked longingly into Aatu's eyes.

He then said, "Now, about my death – I never married, and was never going to be the type of warrior to go off and conquer. And without adding children and land – I worried that respect for me would flee, and taint my family. So, I gave my charge to my cousin. He had recently married and was next in line to inherit. We conspired, and planned for my death by fire. And he secured the post of border guard here for me."

"In the most isolated place of the realm?"

"Well, yeah."

Karaba looked at the nobleman with great regret. Aatu saw her sadness and attempted to liven her mood.

"I see you still have the dragon I gave you."

"Yes, yes I do." She then picked up Aatu's dragon from the table. "And this one is the same."

"Yes, I wanted one just like yours."

"Why?'

"Oh, I just did."

Then Karaba looked intently and seriously into Aatu's eyes. She could see something else, something deeper within him. She grasped his hand tightly, and stated, "No – you made this for a reason. You are not the weak and frivolous boy I thought you once were. You never were. So, tell me, why'd you make it?"

Aatu sighed and took a couple breaths. He wavered and was reluctant to say, for she was his queen and he felt it disrespectful to tell her his feelings, but Karaba was adamant and insisted.

He then spoke meekly, "This dragon I made on your wedding day. Since I couldn't have you, I wanted something to bring me close to you – something that matched what you had. I looked at it each night, before I'd go to sleep – and I hoped that from time to time you might look at yours and think fondly of me."

He paused and lowered his head in shame, expecting Karaba to speak right away, but she didn't. She didn't know what to say. She was consumed in thought – reflecting upon the years that had gone by, and the many times she had thought of him, and wished he had been with her. She was saddened and confused, and felt ashamed that she hadn't been stronger and more honest in her thoughts and behavior. She saw now that Aatu was the strong one – the one whom she had at one time mocked and considered weak and quaint. Aatu had been steady and was the one to show honor. He was a far greater man than her husband, or any of the "worthy suitors", could have ever been.

Aatu lifted his head, and Karaba looked at him with fond and caring eyes, and he could see the sincerity and love in her gaze. She purposefully looked about the room at the various objects and pieces Aatu had created, and then looked back at him and asked softly, "Please tell me about all these things you've made here. I'd like to hear."

And Aatu happily shared with her and explained the many pieces he had made and what he was planning to do.

And she listened carefully, for now she respected and adored him.

the end

CPSIA information can be obtained
at www.ICGtesting.com
Printed in the USA
LVHW031133060919
630096LV00013B/55/P